The True Stor ...omeo

A Very Lucky Connemara Lamb

The True Story of Romeo
A Very Lucky Connemara Lamb

Written and Illustrated by Michele Dunckel

Copyright ©2021 Michele Dunckel

ISBN: 978-1-914488-11-5

This edition printed and bound in the Republic of Ireland by

lettertec

Lettertec Publishing
Springhill House,
Carrigtwohill
Co. Cork
Republic of Ireland
www.selfpublishbooks.ie

For Barb, Michael, The Casey Family
and Killary Sheep Farm

Without them there would be no story.

For Delilah

To Jen —
Best wishes!
M Dunckel

"Hurry up, Michael!" Fiona called over her shoulder as she ran full out toward the trail through the woods. "I've only got half an hour before I have to be home!"

"I'm running as fast as I can," Michael called back, a little out of breath.

"Is your sister coming?" Fiona yelled again as she climbed the gate where the path started.

Michael, who had stopped to catch his breath, replied,"She's on her way. She had to finish her fiddle practice before she could leave." Breath recovered, Michael climbed the gate after Fiona.

"Oh, wow, look at the tree that came down over the path," Fiona said. "We'll have to climb this before we can get to the meadow. Maura should have caught up with us by then."

Just then, they heard a rustling and a thud, followed by, "I'm OK," in Maura's tiny voice. Maura caught up to them moments later. Obstacles behind them, the three raced to the meadow.

"Oooo," Fiona said as the path opened up to reveal a lush field dotted with sheep. "There must be at least three new lambs since we were here yesterday!"

Fiona loved springtime when all the female sheep, called ewes, gave birth to their babies. She and her friends had been coming to this pasture every day after school to count the new lambs. She so wanted to hold one of them, they looked so cuddly! But the ewes quickly scooted their lambs away to keep them safe.

As the three stood admiring the lambs, they heard a very tiny *bah*. They looked at each other and Fiona put her finger to her lips for a silent *shhh*. After a few moments, they heard it again.

Fiona walked quietly in the direction of the sound and peered over an old stone wall. There she saw the tiniest, newborn lamb.

"You guys, look!" she called to her friends as she climbed over the wall. It's a newborn lamb!"

Fiona scooped the lamb into her arms. Finally, she got to hold one! But this one was still damp from the birth. She held the lamb close to keep it warm.

"What are you doing?" Michael asked.

"We can't just leave it here. It'll die without a mother to take care of it," Fiona replied.

"What do you know about taking care of a lamb?" Michael challenged.

Maura spoke up, "What if a fox or a badger comes along to hurt the baby? It's not safe without a mother to protect it. I wonder where its mother could be?"

"I don't know but what are you going to do with it?" Michael repeated his question, and Fiona repeated her statement. "We can't just leave it here."

They were all silent for a moment. Fiona held the lamb a little bit tighter and breathed in its sweet baby smell.

"Let's go," said Fiona.

"Where?" asked Maura.

"We're taking it back to my house. My mother will know what to do."

"You're going to carry it all the way back through the woods?" Michael said, wondering what Fiona was thinking.

"Yes, we are," said Maura, firmly, "and you're going to help."

Maura and Fiona marched back up the path, with Michael trailing behind.

When they got to the fallen tree, Fiona turned to Michael and said, "Here, you hold the lamb while we climb over."

"I don't want to hold it--it's all wet!" Michael exclaimed.

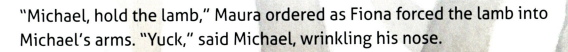

"Michael, hold the lamb," Maura ordered as Fiona forced the lamb into Michael's arms. "Yuck," said Michael, wrinkling his nose.

The girls made Michael hold the lamb again as they climbed over the gate, which Michael found equally distasteful.

Once all three were over the gate and the lamb was back in Fiona's arms, they hurried to Fiona's house. As the house came into sight Maura ran ahead, calling, "Mrs. Flaherty, Mrs. Flaherty! Look what we found!"

Fiona's mother appeared at the open door of her house just as Maura arrived, pointing behind her to where Fiona followed.

"Fiona, what's going on? Whose lamb is that?" her mother asked, with eyes wide and a slight frown.

Quickly, the girls took turns explaining what had happened in the meadow. Michael stood by silently, sure that Fiona would be in trouble. Mrs. Flaherty thought for a moment, then said, "I know what we can do. We can take it up the road to Mr. Casey's farm. I bet he'll know what to do." She grabbed her jacket and the four of them climbed into her car, the lamb still firmly cuddled in Fiona's arms.

Mr. Casey opened his front door as soon as the car pulled into his yard. "Hello," he called, "What have we here?" he asked when he saw Fiona's bundle. Mrs. Flaherty allowed her daughter to tell Mr. Casey the story.

"I'm afraid I can't take in the lamb," Mr. Casey explained. "I don't have a ewe without a baby and this lamb won't survive without a mother of its own. But I know someone who might help. Let me give him a call."

Mr. Casey called his friend Mr. Nee at Killary Sheep Farm. After a short conversation, Mr. Casey said to the group, "Good News! Mr. Nee can take your lamb. Since it's late today, I'll take care of it overnight and you can take it to Mr. Nee in the morning."

The kids cheered and Mrs. Flaherty sighed with relief, "Thank you, Mr. Casey."

"Come on in," Mr. Casey said as he held open the door to his home. "The first thing we have to do is give this little thing some nutrition. Newborn lambs need colostrum, a special milk they usually get from their mothers. I have it here in powder form."

The group watched as Mr. Casey mixed the powder with warm water and filled a bottle, then added a nipple to the top. It was the largest baby bottle the children had ever seen.

Fiona held the lamb and the bottle, trying to get it into the lamb's mouth. The lamb worked very hard to get at the milk, but was just too weak. Mr. Casey took the lamb out of Fiona's arms and skillfully eased a clear plastic tube down its throat. Then he slowly poured the liquid from the bottle into the tube that went directly into the lamb's stomach. Then Mr. Casey passed it back to Fiona. Satisfied with a full tummy, the lamb relaxed against Fiona.

"Okay, let's fix up a place in the barn for this little guy to spend the night." Mr. Casey led them out of the house and down the lane past fields full of ewes with their lambs.

"Mr. Casey, you just called him a 'guy'. Does that mean my lamb is a boy?"

"Yes, Fiona, he's a boy, a Connemara Black Face Sheep," he responded. Then he raised his voice and called, "Kerina, come help us!" When the group arrived at the barn, Kerina was waiting for them. Fiona was very surprised to find that Kerina was only a few years older than she and her friends.

"Kerina, this is Mrs. Flaherty, Fiona, Michael and Maura," Mr. Casey introduced. "They've just rescued this lamb and we're going to help them by taking care of him overnight." Everyone said hello.

"Kerina is very important to our farm," Mr. Casey explained. "She helps deliver the lambs, gives them medication and helps keep them clean. She is also in charge of moving the sheep from field to field so they get healthy green grass to eat,"

"We have a blind sheep who can't be moved with the rest of the flock. We lead her into a sheep trailer and I pull her to the new field on a four-wheeler," Kerina said.

"Wow! You get to drive a four-wheeler?" exclaimed Michael.

"That's a really cool job!" Fiona said.

Mr. Casey and Kerina quickly went about creating a small pen filled with clean, dry straw and hung a heat lamp above it. Then he placed the lamb under the lamp and the baby snuggled into the straw.

"We'll feed him every two hours overnight." Mr. Casey said.

"Thank you so much, Mr. Casey," Fiona said. "We'll see you in the morning."

The group piled back into Mrs. Flaherty's car for the short drive back to Fiona's house.

"I know what his name is," Fiona said.

"Whose name?" Michael asked.

"The lamb's name," Fiona replied impatiently, as she rolled her eyes.
"His name is Romeo," Fiona continued.

"Romeo? What kind of a name is that for a sheep?" Michael asked scornfully.

"The kind I want him to have. I found him, so I get to name him."

"I think Romeo is a great name," Maura said softly.

"Whatever," Michael mumbled.

After they got back to Fiona's house, before Mrs. Flaherty let them out of the car, she turned around so she could face them.

"You three should be very proud of yourselves. You kindly rescued a helpless animal today. Without a mother, he may not survive. But you've given him the best chance possible. I'm proud of all three of you."

"You mean Fiona's not in trouble?" Michael asked.

"Nobody's getting in trouble and you all did a good thing. It's very important to care for nature, animals, as well as the environment. Now get home, you two. Your mum is probably wondering where you are."

With that, Maura and Michael ran in the direction of home, grinning from ear to ear.

The next day, shortly after the sun was up, the three friends climbed into Mrs. Flaherty's car and made the quick trip to Mr. Casey's farm. Romeo had come through the night in great shape. Mr. Casey loaned them a dog crate for the drive to Killary Sheep Farm.

"Thank you, Mr. Casey and Kerina!" the rescuers called as they pulled out of the barnyard.

The drive went quickly until they turned off the main road onto a dirt road that was very narrow. It was hilly and winding, and Fiona was glad there weren't cars coming from the other direction. They came to a sign that read 'Killary Sheep Farm' and then they drove up a steep hill. At the top of the hill was a barn and sheep were everywhere! Fiona's mother had only just gotten out of the car when a man hurried over to meet them.

"Hi, I'm Mr. Nee," he said. "Can I help you?"

"Hi, Mr. Nee. I'm Mrs. Flaherty. Our neighbor, Mr. Casey, called yesterday about taking in a lamb."

"Oh, yes. Welcome! Let's take a look at this guy," Mr. Nee said as he reached into the crate and gathered the baby into his arms.

"I'm Fiona and I found him. His name is Romeo."

"Romeo?" Mr. Nee asked, with a twinkle in his eyes, "That's a fine name! Follow me."

The group followed him into the barn and over to a sink. He gave Romeo back to Fiona as he mixed up a bottle of the same colostrum Mr. Casey had given Romeo the night before.

"Okay, let's see how he does," Mr. Nee said as he handed the bottle to Fiona. Romeo sucked eagerly when he felt the nipple of the bottle against his lips. Fiona grinned as she fed her lamb.

When Romeo was finished, Mr. Nee put him in a stall with ten other lambs who also didn't have mothers. They all huddled together in the clean straw under the heat lamp. Mr. Nee would feed him with a bottle until Romeo was able to eat on his own.

"What is Killary Sheep Farm?" Fiona's mother asked.

"It takes its name from Killary Fjord, the lovely body of water you see around you. My family has raised sheep on this land for 400 years. Now we put on sheep-herding and sheep-shearing demonstrations.

But the best thing we do is rescue lambs. We have visitors from all over the world and they get a chance to pet them and give them bottles. Little Romeo is going to get lots of attention every day. And all of you are welcome to visit anytime you want!"

Fiona couldn't resist climbing into the pen with Romeo to give him one last cuddle and smell again his soft baby coat.

"I'll come visit you as often as my mom lets me!" she whispered in Romeo's ear.

"Fiona, where are you? It's time to go!" Her mother called from the car park.

"I'm coming!" Fiona yelled back, then she gave Romeo a kiss on his head. "Bye bye," she whispered.